The TROUBLE WITH HENRIETTE!

Wende and Harry Devlin

Simon & Schuster Books for Young Readers

SIMON & SCHUSTER BOOKS FOR YOUNG READERS An imprint of Simon & Schuster Children's Publishing Division, 1230 Avenue of the Americas, New York, NY 10020. Copyright © 1995 by Wende and Harry Devlin. All rights reserved including the right of reproduction in whole or in part in any form. SIMON & SCHUSTER BOOKS FOR YOUNG READERS is a trademark of Simon & Schuster. Designed by Christy Hale. The text of this book is set in ITC Garamond Book. The illustrations are rendered in watercolor and ink. Manufactured in Hong Kong by South China Printing Co. (1988) Ltd. 10 9 8 7 6 5 4 3 2 1 Library of Congress Cataloging-in-Publication Data   Devlin, Wende.   The trouble with Henriette / Wende and Harry Devlin.—1st ed.   p.   cm.   Summary: Thinking that Henriette the truffle hound has lost her sense of smell, Jolie's grandfather plans to get rid of her, until she proves her worth in a fancy restaurant in Paris. [1. Dogs—Fiction. 2. Grandfathers—Fiction. 3. Paris (France)—Fiction.] I. Devlin, Harry.   II. Title. PZ7.D49875Tr   1995   [E]—dc20   93-34154   ISBN 0-02-729937-6

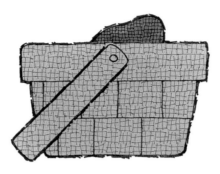

To Madeline Elizabeth Devlin

Grandfather's farm truck sputtered into the big city.
Putt-putt-putt.

Maybe this is the worst day of my life, thought Jolie, squeezed between Grandfather and her truffle hound, Henriette. Jolie hugged Henriette close. Today, she was going to lose her dog.

"The trouble with Henriette," Grandfather had grumbled, "is that she can't find a truffle. A dog must earn her keep on a farm. We will trade her in for a better dog."

Jolie's dark eyes filled with tears. There wasn't a better dog in all of France!

Grandfather had forgotten that Jolie had raised this dog from a thin, not-supposed-to-live puppy and that they had been best friends on a very lonely farm. He had forgotten that he once called Henriette the best truffle hound ever! Henriette had sniffed out hundreds of truffles, those mushroom-like delicacies, under the farm's great oaks, and Grandfather's baskets were always filled.

The trouble was with Grandfather! He wouldn't listen.
Jolie knew why Henriette had lost her sense of smell.
Grandfather had moved Henriette from Jolie's bedroom to
the barn to keep the fox away from the chickens. From that
day on, red-eyed and sneezing, Henriette had slept the
hours away.

"She has hay fever. The barn is dusty and cold. She misses me," cried Jolie.

"Poppycock!" said Grandfather scornfully. "Henriette must go."

Putt-putt-putt. Grandfather slowed his truck to a stop in front of the dazzling Hotel Éclair, the finest in all of Paris. Red velvet curtains filled the windows, and soft light from crystal chandeliers gleamed in the fancy rooms.

The hotel door was open. Music and the fragrance of wondrous foods filled the air.

"Ah, the finest in all of Paris!" Grandfather sighed. "Look, Jolie, that's where I used to sell my truffles when I had a *good* truffle hound."

Henriette sat up. Away from the barn, she seemed to come alive. She put her nose out the window.

Henriette's tail wagged, she trembled, she whined, and with a mighty leap, she sprang out of the truck and ran straight to the doorway of the Hotel Éclair.

Through the doorman's legs she scrambled, with Jolie
and Grandfather in close pursuit. Henriette was loose in the
Hotel Éclair!

"Help! A hound dog in the Hotel Éclair!" gasped the
doorman. His hat flew off as he chased the dog through
the lobby.

Frantic, the desk clerk rang his bell.

Henriette the truffle hound sniffed wildly and galloped
into the dining room. Women screamed. A waiter spun and
lost a fine cheese soufflé.

Skidding into a pastry cart, Henriette sent gooseberry tarts and fudge cakes sailing through the air. A whipped-cream banana pie landed in a woman's lap.

Henriette slid to a stop and, to everyone's horror, settled her nose in Count Maurice's dish of truffles and cream. Her tail wagged furiously. Triumph! Truffles!

Count Maurice! A huge, stern man with a red mustache.
Count Maurice! The hotel's most important guest. Jolie
held her breath. She stared at the count's ruined dinner.
Disaster!

"I'm sorry, sir … You see, Henriette is a truffle hound."

Count Maurice rumbled to his feet, napkin in hand.
"Harrumph!" he announced.
A hush fell over the room.

Count Maurice scowled and glared about. He saw a
frightened girl, a shaking Grandfather, and a truffle hound
whose only sin was to find his truffles. The count was a
gentleman.

"A toast!" he commanded. "To an amazing—a most splendid—truffle hound! Amid all these feasts, she found my truffles. To Henriette! To our flag! To our country!" He raised his glass.

Uncertainly, the other guests rose and lifted their glasses, too.

Jolie wiped the cream from Henriette's nose with the count's napkin. Grandfather scooped the hound up in his arms and, with a farmer's pride, walked grandly out of the Hotel Éclair.

"She is not for sale," he announced to the doorman.

It was a happy ride back to the old farmhouse. All the way home, Jolie hugged her dog.

Finally, Grandfather turned to Jolie. "I'm sorry. You were right about the hay fever. Henriette *is* a splendid truffle hound. From now on, she will sleep in your room." Grandfather had learned how important it was to listen to his granddaughter.

So Henriette became a great truffle hound again.
Grandfather's baskets were filled, and the Hotel Éclair
bought all the precious truffles Henriette could find.

Now quite often, in that very same Hotel Éclair, you can find Jolie and Grandfather eating strawberry pie. Henriette is always left at home. That was a promise made to a doorman, the head waiter, three bellboys, and the noble Count Maurice.